KULL
THE CAVE CRAWLER

With special thanks to Tabitha Jones

For Sam Fadden

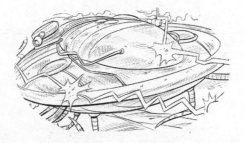

www.seaquestbooks.co.uk

ORCHARD BOOKS
Carmelite House
50 Victoria Embankment
London EC4Y 0DZ

A Paperback Original
First published in Great Britain in 2015

Series created by Beast Quest Limited, London

Text © Beast Quest Limited 2015
Cover and inside illustrations by Artful Doodlers,
with special thanks to Bob and Justin © Orchard Books 2015

A CIP catalogue record for this book is available from
the British Library.

ISBN 978 1 40833 483 6

1 3 5 7 9 10 8 6 4 2

Printed and bound by CPI Group (UK) Ltd, Croydon, CR0 4YY

MIX
Paper from
responsible sources
FSC® C104740

The paper and board used in this book are made from wood
from responsible sources.

Orchard Books is an imprint of Hachette Children's Group
and published by The Watts Publishing Group Limited,
an Hachette UK company.

www.hachette.co.uk

KULL
THE CAVE CRAWLER

BY ADAM BLADE

ORCHARD

SIBORG'S HIVE LOG

DESTINATION: AQUORA

A plague is coming to Aquora!

Max and that pathetic Merryn girl
think they have defeated me, but
I have only become stronger. I
have analysed Max's weakness –
his love for his family! And soon
I will take from him all that he
holds dear.

I will do something my weak
father, the so-called Professor,
never could. Take over Aquora! And
I won't even need to fire a single
shot. The city will be mine, and
everyone in it my slaves!

Max couldn't have dreamt up the
horror I have in store for him,
even in his worst nightmares...

CHAPTER ONE

THE SEA OF FIRE

Max could see nothing but shadowy darkness whizzing past the watershield as the aquafly zoomed westwards. He was pushing the sub as fast as it would go, but still, coils of dread twisted in his stomach like restless snakes. *Everyone I care about is depending on me this time*, Max thought.

He looked into his rear viewer. The sun was rising over Delta Quadrant, casting a fiery glow through the ocean. Above the craft, the surface of the water shone like burnished copper. *The Sea of Fire*, Max thought. It was certainly living up to its name. And the dim, smouldering light below the waves matched Max's mood precisely.

He could just make out the dark silhouettes of his dogbot Rivet and his best friend Lia's swordfish, Spike, swimming close to the craft. The sight of Spike without Lia on his back made Max feel gloomier than ever. But he knew that if Lia were with them now, she would be trying to kill him. She had been infected with one of Max's enemy Siborg's mindbugs, and Max just couldn't shake the memory of her hate-filled eyes the last time he'd seen her.

I'm not going to let Siborg hurt her! Max promised himself. *But right now, the only way I can help Lia is to reach the Professor's secret lab as fast as I can. That is, if I can trust him to keep his word…*

Max glanced at his uncle. The Professor was sitting beside him and craned forwards, squinting through the watershield into the gloom.

"How far now?" Max asked him.

The Professor leaned back and sighed. "Patience, Max, patience," he said. "As I told you the last ten times you asked, if we keep heading west, we will reach my lab before long."

Max gritted his teeth. "It's not easy to be patient when a power-crazed lunatic is holding your mum hostage and controlling your dad and best friend like a pair of evil puppets! And you said yourself, if we don't destroy Siborg's mindbugs soon, it will be too late. You might not care if your son turns the whole population of Aquora into mindless robots for good, but I'm not going to let that happen!"

"Oh Max, you underrate me terribly," the Professor said. "Of course I care. I care immensely. After all, I'm not likely to get my official pardon if my maniac son remains in control."

Max scowled, his temper flaring. *My uncle only cares about himself!* he thought, wiping a

film of sweat from his forehead. *And why is it so hot in here?* Max jabbed at the controls for the cooling system, then took a deep breath, turning his attention back to the brightening seascape before them.

As the sun rose higher, the view began to open up. Max could see that the seabed below was made from black pumice – rock formed by cooling lava, pitted all over with shallow holes. It twisted into strange folds and narrow ravines. Bulbous rock formations reached up towards the surface and columns of bubbling gases shone amber in the fiery light. Then Max spotted something that made him jolt upright in his seat. The black seabed ahead was laced with glimmering orange cracks.

"Whoa!" Max said, hitting the brakes. "That's lava!"

The Professor chuckled. "No cause for alarm," he said. "We're safe enough. We've just reached the border between the Delta and the Gamma Quadrants. I'm surprised you didn't realise it was an active fault. Why else did you think this area was called the Sea of Fire?"

Max glowered at his uncle. "I thought it was just a name," he said. "Like the Emerald Sea. I wasn't expecting actual fire." Max eased forward the thrust lever, swallowing his irritation as he steered between two lumpy columns of rock. Working with his evil uncle was really starting to take its toll. *But I have no choice*, he told himself for the hundredth time. The Professor had the Merryn Touch like Max and his mother, which meant that unlike everyone else in Aquora, they were immune to Siborg's mindbugs. He also had a weapon hidden in a secret lab that could destroy the horrible robotic insects that had infected the population. *Or that's what he said, anyway...*

The Professor waved a hand towards

the rocky seascape. "Of course," he said, "technically, there is no actual fire. Just molten rock and geothermal vents. Even so, this is still one of the most fascinating areas of Nemos. There are deposits of volcanic ash filled with fossils. And living fossils too – ancient relics from long ago that still hunt these waters. All in all, an exceptional place to design evil Robobeasts."

Max clenched his teeth. "Look, can we have a bit less about evil robots and just focus on getting hold of this raygun and getting back to Aquora?" he said.

The Professor shrugged. "If you wish," he said, settling himself back in his seat. "And in fact, my raygun is a rather fascinating subject. You, know, if I'd ever got it finished, I think it would have been even more powerful than my son's tech-disrupter ray."

Unlikely, Max thought. As far as he could

tell, Siborg's evil inventions were in a whole different league to the Professor's. But before Max could speak, Rivet's voice came through his headset, sounding strangely distorted.

"Hot, Max!" Rivet barked. "Feel funny, Max!" Max glanced at his dogbot in the rear viewer and saw that Rivet and Spike were both starting to lag behind. Spike's eyes looked glazed, and his fins were moving sluggishly. *He looks terrible*, Max thought. The streams of swirling black and orange lava were running directly below them now and it was so hot, Max's deepsuit was stuck to his body with sweat. He checked the external thermometer display, and felt a jolt of alarm. *This ocean's like a hot tub!*

"Max!" Rivet barked urgently. "Need help, Max!" The dogbot bleeped, then let out a stream of robotic gibberish.

"Hang on, Riv!" Max said. "I'm coming."

He turned to the Professor. "We need to stop so I can fix Rivet."

The Professor frowned. "I thought we were in a hurry," he said.

"We are!" Max said. "But I'm not leaving Rivet behind!"

The Professor sighed. "Oh, really," he said. "For some reason my obsession with robots is considered unhealthy, while it's fine for you to dote on that dogbot as if it were a real animal."

Max glared at the Professor. "Rivet's a highly sophisticated artificial intelligence, and he's saved my life more times than I can count. And anyway, there's a big difference between looking after your robots, like I do, and trying to take over the world with them, like you do!"

"Fine," the Professor said. "Let's stop. But be quick. It's your parents we're racing to save, remember."

As if I could forget! Max slammed the

aquafly to a stop, flipped the lid, and swam out into the sweltering water. He could see immediately that Rivet was in a bad way. He was panting, and his red eyes were barely glowing at all. Max opened the panel in his dogbot's side and adjusted the thermostat to ramp up his cooling system. Then he turned to poor Spike. The swordfish's skin had lost its healthy sheen and his eyes looked dull and listless.

"Oh, Spike," Max said. "We'll get you out of this hot water soon. And I'm doing everything I can to help Lia, I promise." Max reached a hand towards the swordfish's back, but Spike shied out of reach, clicking softly. Then suddenly his eyes went wide, and he flicked his tail, darting away at full speed.

"Spike!" Max called. "Come back!" But Spike surged onwards through the bubbling water. *I have to stop him*, Max thought. *I can't*

lose him! Lia would be devastated.

"Max! Get back in here!" the Professor called. "We need to get to my lab!"

Max shook his head. "We can't leave without Spike," he said. Max grabbed his dogbot round the waist. "Follow Spike!"

Max's stomach lurched as Rivet powered through the water after the speeding swordfish.

CHAPTER TWO

AN UNWELCOME APPEARANCE

Max kicked hard, adding his power to Rivet's as they swooped over the craggy seascape. Spike was losing them fast, swerving between pillars of volcanic rock.

"Spike! Wait!" Max called, but the swordfish didn't even look back. Streams of black-flecked lava flowed across the seabed, making the water shimmer with heat. As Max squinted ahead, a burst of overheated exhaust jetted from Rivet's rear right into his face. Max grimaced. "Rivet!"

"Sorry, Max!" Rivet barked. "Can't help it, Max." The dogbot's thrusters were firing at full throttle, but Spike was getting further ahead by the moment. *Where on Nemos is that swordfish going?* Max wondered. *I hope he's not off to find Lia –*

"Max!" The Professor's voice suddenly blared through his headset. "I can see something on the scanner. And it's heading towards you, fast. No…hang on…make that several somethings."

Max's stomach clenched with dread. "Spike!" he called one last time. But the swordfish darted out of view behind a ridge in the ocean floor. Max could already hear the high-pitched whine of engines. He turned to see five sleek hydrodisks zooming towards him. The wings of each craft were decorated with Aquora's military emblem, but Siborg's scarlet eye had been daubed over the top. Behind their watershields Max could see more scarlet eyes peering at him. *Cyrates!*

The hydrodisks came to an abrupt halt and a chorus of robotic voices echoed through the water. "Freeze! Or we will open fire."

"Whoa, Riv!" Max cried, letting go of his dogbot and using his arms and legs to stop.

The Professor pulled up alongside him in the aquafly. Max's uncle shook his head behind the craft's viewing screen. "Why do you never listen?"

A flickering image was forming before the lead hydrodisk, beamed from a device above its watershield. Max felt sick as the 3D projection became clear. It showed the dining table in Max's apartment. Callum, Max's father, was serving pancakes onto a plate. Behind the plate, knife and fork at

the ready, sat Siborg. He was lounging in his chair, dressed in a military jumpsuit, and smiling like the cat who'd got the cream. Max's mother, Niobe, was squirming in the seat beside Siborg, bound and gagged. Max swallowed the sick feeling in his throat as the image of Siborg turned towards him.

"Greetings, cousin," came Siborg's voice through Max's headset. "I must say, I'm

enjoying living your life immensely. Having a
real father instead of a pathetic failed inventor
is rather novel. And soon I'll have a mother
too. My work on developing a mindbug to
infect those with the Merryn Touch is coming
along nicely. Which makes your little 'Quest'
rather pointless, doesn't it?" Siborg flashed
Max a smile. "Why don't you come home to
Mummy and Daddy like a good little boy?"

Max glared at the image of his cousin, rage boiling inside him. Finally, he shook his head. "You're crazy!" Max said. "Taking over Aquora so you can steal my parents? You seriously need some help. But I'm not going to let you get away with it."

Siborg shrugged. "Suit yourself," he said. "I hope you enjoy your last moments." Then he popped a bit of pancake into his mouth and turned back to his meal. As the image started to fade Max saw that the blaster cannons of all five hydrodisks were swivelling towards him.

The Professor swung the aquafly around and raced away towards a craggy underwater mountain. "Riv, go!" Max cried. He grabbed hold of his dogbot's waist, clinging tight as Rivet dived into the aquafly's slipstream.

ZAP! An energy bolt zoomed past them, smashing into a pillar of rock and blasting it to pieces. Max spat out a mouthful of gritty water as they sped through the debris, then glanced behind him. Another energy bolt was headed their way. "Hard left!" Max cried. The Professor swerved through an arch of twisted rock. Rivet kept pace behind the aquafly while Max held on tight, kicking with all his strength.

"Max!" the Professor called through his intercom. "We're almost at my base. See that volcano up ahead?" Max nodded. They were fast approaching the flat-topped mountain that Max had spotted in the distance, and now he could see the water above it was shimmering with heat. "My lab's inside," the Professor went on. "Once we reach the top, I can activate its defences. Full speed ahead!"

Rivet's engines growled as he raced to keep up with the aquafly. Max put every bit of power he had into kicking his legs, but he could hear the throb of the cyrates' hydrodisks getting louder by the moment. As they approached the Professor's lab, Max felt a pang of unease. *I'm racing right into my uncle's lair!* he thought. But then another energy bullet zapped past him, and Max pushed the thought from his mind. *It's got to be safer in there than out here!*

The seabed rose steeply as they reached the base of the volcano. The aquafly banked upwards, and Rivet climbed through the water on its tail. Suddenly a deafening sound echoed through the water behind them.

VROOM! Max glanced back and a jolt of adrenaline seared through him. The biggest torpedo he'd ever seen was rocketing through the water towards him. *It's going to hit us!*

"Sharp right!" Max cried. Rivet jerked to the side, and Max almost lost his grip on his dogbot's sides with the force of the turn.

The giant torpedo sped past, swirling Max and Rivet around in its current.

BANG! A shower of broken rock exploded from the side of the volcano as the missile ploughed into it. A moment later, a wall of water and fragments of stone slammed into Max's body. His hands were torn from Rivet's sides, and he tumbled over and over, his chest

and legs throbbing with bruises. He caught a glimpse of his aquafly spinning through the water nearby, and Rivet spiralling away from him, caught up in the blast.

Finally, the swirling water grew calm, and Max swam to a stop. Grit drifted around him, but through the cloudy water, Max could see Rivet and the aquafly nearby, and the volcano rising up straight ahead. From behind, he could still hear the whir of the hydrodisks' engines. He turned to see their white lights powering towards him, and through their watershields, the glowing red eyes of the cyrates. The water before the hydrodisks flickered, and a giant hologram of Siborg's half-metal face glared through the debris.

"You know what, Max?" Siborg said. "Your tireless heroics are really starting to get on my nerves." There was an electronic hum and all five hydrodisks aimed their glinting guns towards Max. "It's time to put an end to you once and for all," Siborg said.

CHAPTER THREE

THE CAVE CRAWLER

Max balled his fists as he looked through the image of his cousin's grinning face at the arsenal of guns aimed towards him. *I'm not going down without a fight!* he thought. He turned and locked eyes with the Professor through the watershield of the aquafly. The Professor nodded. "Attack!" Max cried.

Max heard a whirring sound from the aquafly as the Professor aimed the acid torpedoes. Rivet let out a growl and lunged forwards just as the ocean around Max flashed red with blaster fire.

Max kicked upwards, dodging the energy bolts, then darted toward the nearest hydrodisk. Rivet had already sunk his sharp teeth into the wing of the neighbouring sub, and was tearing away a chunk of metal. Max lifted his hyperblade and lashed it across the watershield of the hydrodisk before him, then leaned through the shattered glass towards the evil robot inside. The cyrate swiped a metal fist towards Max's face, but Max ducked, then swung his hyperblade again.

Swish! His blade sliced through the robot's neck, severing its head from its body. As the cyrate's body sagged Max yanked it from its seat and tossed it away, then darted through the broken watershield.

"Here, Riv!" Max cried.

"Coming, Max!" Rivet spun and powered towards the hydrodisk, then leapt into the seat beside Max. Another hydrodisk was already swerving towards them, so Max grabbed the controls and dived, just as blasts of red energy erupted above. He steered sharply upwards, sending his hydrodisk round in a tight loop. Water whooshed through the broken watershield, making the vessel judder, but he managed to keep his seat against the sloshing water. Once the enemy hydrodisk was in his sights, he opened fire.

ZAP! His energy bolt hit the sub at point-blank range and the craft exploded into a starburst of glittering metal and glass. Max grinned with satisfaction as he surged away. He spotted the Professor, steering the aquafly in and out of cracks in the side of the volcano with two enemy craft on his tail. The last hydrodisk was nowhere to be seen. Max hit the accelerator, climbing the mountain towards the Professor and aiming his blasters at the cyrates.

CRASH! Max was thrown forwards in his seat as an energy bolt hit his hydrodisk from behind. Rivet was thrown against the dashboard, and everything started to spin. Water swirled around Max, snatching the breath from his gills. He glanced into his rear viewer and spotted the final cyrate's hydrodisk zooming away. Ahead, the side of the volcano was rushing towards him at deadly speed.

"Time to get out!" Max cried to Rivet, then he kicked upwards and out through the broken watershield. Rivet whizzed to his side just as their discarded hydrodisk smashed into the volcano with a boom that seemed to shake the whole seabed.

At the same moment, a huge shadow fell across them. Max looked up, and froze. An oval creature the size of a tanker was hovering above him. Curved antennae shimmering with a strange blue light swept backwards from the creature's vast, domed head. Its massive body was covered with interlocking armour plates with thorn-like spikes jutting sideways into the water, and a row of pointed legs ran along each of its sides. *A trilobite?* Max thought. *But they're extinct!* Talons of fear clutched hold of his chest and squeezed as he realised that the blue sheen on the creature's antennae was created by a network of glowing wires. *It's one of Siborg's Robobeasts!*

"Cyrate, Max!" Rivet barked. Max turned to find the cyrate sub surging back towards him, guns aimed and ready. Max swallowed hard. He could now make out every detail of the cyrate's skeletal face. His mind raced, but with the volcano behind him and the Robobeast above, there was no escape. *This is it!* Max clenched his muscles and held his breath as the cyrate's eyes burned brighter and the throb of engines filled his ears…

Suddenly a jagged tongue of blue electricity hit the hydrodisk with a sharp crack. The sub juddered and sizzled, and Max could see the robot pilot inside convulsing, its red eyes flashing wildly. Max looked up to see that the trilobite had extended one of its long antennae, and the bolt of electricity was coming from the tip. As the electricity fizzled away, the hydrodisk fell through the water and tumbled down the side of the volcano, leaving a trail of bubbles.

Max couldn't believe it. *I'm alive.*

"Ha ha!" the Professor's voice cackled gleefully through Max's headset. "Meet Kull the Cave Crawler! One of my earliest inventions and still one of my best. It's built using an ancient creature that only survives here, in the Sea of Fire. And it follows my instructions to the letter. Kull! Destroy the cyrates!"

The huge trilobite's body curled, then flexed. Max gasped as it shot through the water at astonishing speed towards the aquafly and the remaining hydrodisks on its trail. As Kull approached, one of the cyrates spun and fired a volley of energy bolts at the ancient creature, but they bounced off Kull's thick armour without leaving a mark. A bolt of electricity zigzagged from Kull's antenna and hit the hydrodisk with an ear-splitting crack. The hydrodisk sparked and dropped like a stone. The massive trilobite turned and

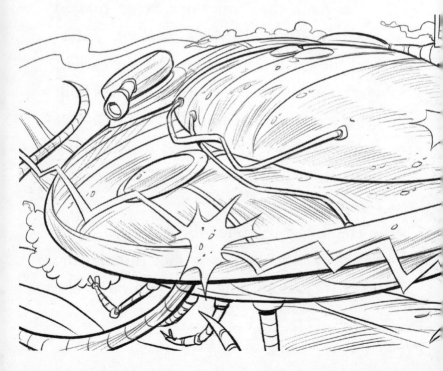

swooped towards its next target, which had abandoned the aquafly, and was whizzing away through the water.

"Look at it go!" the Professor cried.

But the sound of his voice was cut off by a crackling transmission coming through on Max's headset. "I wouldn't break out the party hats just yet," Siborg said, his sneering voice sending a shiver down Max's spine.

"Your primitive Robobeast may have saved you for now, but there are plenty more cyrates where those came from, and they're heading your way. Fast."

As Kull drew close to the final cyrate, it curled its flexible body into a ball, then flicked its tail.

BAM! The tail smashed into the hydrodisk, sending it spinning away through the water until it crashed into a rock and crumpled flat. The crackling in Max's headset stopped. Siborg's minions, his eyes and ears, were defeated. *For now at least.*

Max scanned the smouldering shadows around the volcano and felt a pang of guilt. *Spike's still out here somewhere. But where?*

"Max!" the Professor called, zooming towards him in the aquafly, "Jump aboard!" He flipped the cockpit open as he swooped in close. Max shook himself. *The sooner we get that raygun, the sooner we can find Spike, and save Lia.* "Come on, Riv!" he said, and dived into the aquafly beside his uncle.

Once Rivet and Max were inside, the Professor closed the cockpit and lifted the nose of the craft. "You could have warned me you had a Robobeast here!" Max said to his uncle.

"I'll take that as a thank you," replied the Professor, pulling back on the control stick. They climbed the side of the volcano, keeping just above the pitted rock.

When they came to a narrow cleft, the Professor angled the aquafly through the gap towards a hidden metal door. Then he muttered something into his headset, and the door slid silently open, revealing an orange glow within. Max blinked in the light, trying to see inside. *The Professor's secret lab*, he thought, as a tingle ran down his spine.

CHAPTER FOUR

THE SECRET LAB

Max was hit by a stifling wave of heat as the Professor guided the aquafly inside an airlock carved into the mountainside. The small space was lit only by glowing cracks in the cavern walls. At another command from the Professor, the airlock's external door slid closed and the water started to drain away. Once the water was gone, Max opened the aquafly's cockpit. He almost choked. The air was hot and humid, and stank of rotten eggs.

"Smelly, Max!" Rivet barked.

The Professor glanced at Rivet and raised an eyebrow. "What remarkable powers of perception your pet robot has," he told Max.

"Actually," Max said, covering his nose with his hand, "Rivet's sense of smell is thousands of times more powerful than ours. Which is something I seriously don't envy him right now."

Max opened a panel in the dashboard before him, and took out the glowing piece of crystal they'd found in the Howling Caves. He slipped it into his pocket, and they all hopped out of the aquafly, their feet clattering on the airlock's metal meshwork floor.

A doorway ahead of them opened, and even more foul air wafted out. Max wrinkled his nose as the Professor led them into a large, square room. The walls were a patchwork of rusting grey metal, bundled wires and corroding pipes. Ancient-looking black and white monitors with oversized levers and knobs were built into the walls, and the room was muggy and swelteringly hot.

Max grimaced. "This is where you work?" he said. "You could at least have installed some air conditioning."

The Professor scowled. "I'll have you know that some of my greatest inventions have come out of this lab," he said. "It's been up and running since you were in nappies. And anyway, this is only the security room. Follow me." The Professor led Max and Rivet across a metal floor that echoed underfoot. He stopped in front of a stained and pock-marked door and tapped a code into a control panel. Max felt a twinge of unease. *If the Professor changes sides now, Riv and I will be well and truly trapped.* The door before him slid open, and red light flooded out. Max followed his uncle inside.

"Wow!" Max felt a lurching vertigo as he found himself in a glass corridor suspended high above the volcano's crater. Far below, a thin crust of black molten rock, laced with

orange cracks, swirled and churned. As Max watched, bubbles of magma formed and burst, belching out plumes of steam and noxious gases. He stared in awe at the hypnotic movement.

"I see you are more impressed now," the Professor said. "All in all, I think you'll agree this is a marvellous location for creating robotic beasts. The lava in the volcano provides a constant source of energy for forging my inventions."

Max dragged his eyes away from the magma and shook the afterimage from his vision, suddenly sickened at the thought of all the sea creatures who must have suffered here at his uncle's hands.

"Marvellous isn't the word I would use," Max muttered. "Evil and twisted, more like."

The Professor shrugged, and led Max and Rivet onwards through the tube and into an

enormous room, where a glass wall at the back gave a view of the crater below. The other walls were all of natural black rock, and on the far side of the room, a series of oval windows overlooked a dark expanse of pumice scattered with rusting hulks of metal. Shelves, desks and some more modern flat-screen monitors were built into the walls of the lab. Max could see blueprints on some

of the monitors, and spinning holographic
models projected above the desks. He
recognised many of them as Robobeasts he'd
defeated. Cephalox the Cyber Squid, Silda
the Electric Eel, Manak the Silent Predator…
all evil Robobeasts created from enslaved
animals and designed to kill. Max could feel
a terrible anger welling up inside him. His
head was starting to throb.

He turned away from the monitors and crossed to one of the windows that looked out onto the dark plain scattered with metallic debris. He noticed with disgust that each chunk of metal looked like a misshapen animal part.

"That's where I build my robots," the Professor said, arriving at his shoulder and gazing out over the bleak view.

Hot blood surged into Max's face as his anger boiled over. "You mean that's where you force innocent sea creatures like Kull to do your evil bidding," Max said.

The Professor chuckled. "Interesting you should see it that way when Kull just saved your life," he said. "Anyway, I think that's enough preaching from you. We should find that raygun and get going before my son becomes your adopted brother forever." Max shuddered at the thought of Siborg at home with his parents. He took a deep breath to calm himself, but there just wasn't enough air. He balled his fists instead, and turned away from his uncle.

Rivet scampered to his side. "Rivet help Max find raygun!" the dogbot barked, wagging his tail. Max patted Rivet's head, grateful for the distraction.

"So what are we looking for?" Max asked his uncle, once he'd started to feel a bit calmer.

"A red and yellow gun, about this big," the Professor said, holding his hands shoulder-width apart. "I created it to disrupt certain types of electrical circuit. On its own, it wouldn't be nearly powerful enough to destroy the mindbugs, but the crystal we picked up in the Howling Caves should amplify the signal."

"What do you mean by *should*?" Max

SEA QUEST

asked. "I thought you were sure?"

"As sure as I can be," the Professor said, "but before I can modify the gun we need to find it, and the only cleaner I ever persuaded to work here left years ago after I slightly modified her pet cat. So, off you go."

Max shook his head in disbelief. Then he started to pick his way around the room, running his eyes over the cluttered desks and shelves. Everything was covered in a thick layer of black volcanic dust, and starting to turn red with rust.

"Play, Max!" Rivet suddenly barked, his nose pointed towards a black metal stick on a low shelf. Max crossed to his dogbot's side and reached his hand out, wanting to take a closer look at the stick.

"No!" the Professor shouted. "Don't touch that." Max snatched his hand back. "That's a stunstick," the Professor explained. "It's very old and very powerful. I really have no idea what damage it would do to you."

Max sighed and continued his search of the room. Everything he saw looked ancient, and he found himself starting to seriously doubt that the Professor could help him at all.

"Found it, Max!" Rivet barked from across the room. He'd opened a cabinet, and was nosing at a red and yellow gun inside, his tail wagging happily.

"Good boy, Riv," Max said, crossing to Rivet's side. Max reached into the cabinet and took out the gun. It felt reassuringly solid and heavy.

"Can I have the gun over here please?" the Professor called from a nearby desk. "I'll need you to hold it steady while I rejig a couple of circuits to accommodate the crystal."

Max laid the gun on the desk, and held it

still while the Professor used a slim tool to open a panel in its side, revealing an intricate pattern of wires, chips and beam-forming lenses.

As Max glanced at the workings of the raygun, he was relieved to see that although the technology was old, the design was clever. The Professor got to work snipping wires and soldering new connections while Max held the weapon steady.

"Right," the Professor said finally, pointing at a small space in the circuitry. "If you could slot the crystal in there, I'll make a couple more tweaks, and then I think we'll be just about ready to start zapping mindbugs." Max carefully slid the glowing green stone into the gun, but as it clicked into place, he heard the swish of an electric door opening. The Professor sprang away from him with a cry of alarm.

"Freeze!" a familiar voice snarled from behind them. Max spun around to see a slim figure standing in the doorway wearing an Amphibio mask and aiming a blaster at his head.

"Lia!" Max cried.

CHAPTER FIVE

A DEADLY DILEMMA

"New and improved," Lia said, smiling nastily as she glared at him down the barrel of her gun.

"How did you get in here?!" the Professor snapped.

"Your pet trilobite was busy chasing cyrates," Lia told him. Her lips moved as she spoke, but the voice that came from her throat was twisted and distorted into Siborg's monotone. Hearing Siborg's voice from Lia's lips filled Max with horror.

"He didn't seem interested in your little Merryn friend at all," Lia went on. "And your password was pathetically easy to guess. My birthday? How sweet. It almost makes me feel bad about having to kill you. But let's cut to the chase." Lia tossed her silver hair and narrowed her eyes. "Hand me that raygun," she said. Max could see her finger tightening on the trigger of her blaster. "Now!"

Max stared at Lia, fighting to control the emotions swirling inside him. Her eyes glinted coldly as she glared back at him down the barrel of the blaster. Max shook his head. "I can't do that," he said.

Lia shrugged. "I thought you might say that," she said. Then she smiled coldly, and pulled the trigger of her gun. Max dropped to the floor. Lia's energy bullet whizzed over his head, hitting a metal table with a *ping* before ricocheting around the room. As Max scrambled to his feet, he saw that Lia had turned her gun on his uncle, who was cowering against a wall.

Lia strode across the room and pressed the muzzle to the side of the Professor's head. The Professor's eyes shot wide open and he slowly raised his hands.

Lia turned to Max. "Now, give her the gun or I kill this worthless specimen," Siborg's voice said.

Max glanced towards his uncle, standing stiff and frozen in Lia's grasp. The Professor met his gaze and carefully mouthed the words "Give it to her!"

Max was tempted to turn and run. Maybe he could escape while Lia was dealing with the Professor. The raygun was almost ready. He'd be able to finish it and save his parents.

But at the sight of his uncle, helpless and afraid, Max felt the tug of reality. He just couldn't do it. He couldn't let Siborg kill him. The Professor was a human being, even if he was evil. Besides, Max couldn't leave Lia. His whole body felt heavy with defeat as he closed the side of the raygun and tossed it to the Merryn princess.

She snatched the gun deftly from the

air, while still holding her blaster to the Professor's head.

"Touching." Siborg's voice echoed from Lia's lips. "If you weren't so utterly pathetic you'd have let this snivelling waste of space die. And of course," Lia's face twisted into a horrible smile as Siborg went on, "there really is nothing to stop me getting your Merryn friend to kill him now anyway."

Lia aimed a sharp kick at the back of the Professor's knees, sending him sprawling. The Professor struggled as Lia shoved her foot in the small of his back, but Max knew how strong Siborg's mindbugs made their victims. The Professor didn't have a chance. As Lia shifted her aim back to the Professor's head, Max knew he had to do something, and quickly. *But what?*

Suddenly, he heard the scrabble of metal paws, and the next moment Rivet was flying through the air towards Lia. The dogbot slammed into her side just as her blaster fired. She staggered sideways, her energy bolt glancing off the metal floor right beside the Professor's head. *Nice one, Rivet!* The Professor yelped and rolled sideways, then scrambled to his feet. Max's dogbot barked and lunged for Lia's leg, but Lia kicked out, sending the dogbot flying. Rivet hit the ground with a thunk, then clambered up and shook himself.

Max heard the electric hum of Lia's blaster recharging as she turned and took aim at the dogbot. Max knew he only had moments to act. Then he remembered – *The stunstick!* He covered the distance to where it lay in three long strides, snatched it up and spun, racing across the lab towards Lia. She turned, aiming her blaster towards him, but Max lunged, and before she could fire he

pressed the trigger of the stunstick, sending a crackling blue bolt out towards her.

BAM! Lia's body stiffened, outlined by a flickering blue light. Then she crumpled to the ground and lay twitching, her eyelids closed.

Max fell to her side and felt her pulse, his chest tight with worry. Rivet nudged Lia with his nose. Only when Max felt a strong, steady beat did he let himself breathe again. He gently prised the raygun from Lia's webbed fingers and slipped it into his belt.

"Enemy craft approaching!" A mechanical female voice rang out from the base's loudspeakers.

"We're under attack!" the Professor said. "The girl will live. She's only stunned, but we have to get out of here now!"

Max bent and lifted Lia, bundling her unconscious body over his shoulder.

"Surely you're not thinking of bringing her with us?" the Professor said. "She tried to kill me!"

"That wasn't Lia. It was Siborg," Max said, "and I'm not going anywhere without her. We just need to fix the raygun, then we can use it to destroy her mindbug and set her free."

The Professor sighed. "I suppose we will

need to test the gun," he said, "but let's hurry! If she wakes up while you're carrying her you're in trouble. She packs a surprising punch for a little girl."

"Rivet! Back to the aquafly!" Max told his dogbot. Lia's slim form joggled up and down on Max's shoulder as they raced along the glass corridor that spanned the bubbling crater. The Professor opened the door to the airlock, and clambered into the aquafly. Max lifted Lia gently into her seat, then leapt in beside her, stowing the raygun and stunstick under the dashboard. Rivet bounded onto his lap and Max closed the cockpit roof.

The ocean doors parted, letting in a swirl of water. As soon as they were submerged Max gunned the engines and zoomed out of the volcano into the sea.

Right away, Max could see the huge, black form of Kull hovering ahead, feelers twitching and black eyes glinting.

"Excellent!" the Professor said. "Kull should deal with any cyrates on our tail!"

Max started to steer around the mighty trilobite, but as the aquafly zoomed past, Kull flicked its legs and tail, blocking the way.

"Move, you big oaf!" the Professor snapped into his headset, but Kull stayed where it was, its huge black eyes staring fixedly at the sub.

"I think you'll find Kull's not quite as friendly as it used to be," Lia said, speaking in Siborg's robotic voice. Max turned to see her pushing herself up on her elbow, looking wide awake and smug. "I did a bit of tinkering before I joined you in the lab."

"You stole my Robobeast!" the Professor cried.

Lia smirked. "And it was far too easy," she said.

Max felt a stab of horror. He turned his

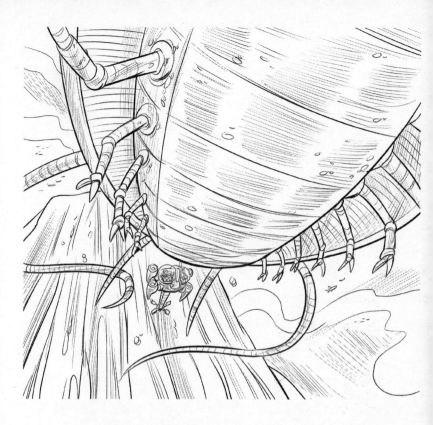

attention back to the huge, armoured shape
before him, and his stomach clenched as
he saw a blue electric current crackling
along Kull's antennae. Suddenly the massive
Robobeast flicked its body, and its ram-like
head swooped toward them.

CHAPTER SIX

THE HEART OF THE VOLCANO

As Max tugged the controls, steering them out of the giant creature's path, Lia's hand whipped forward and hit the release for the exit hatch. It flipped open, slowing the aquafly with a jolt that flung Max against the dashboard. The Professor and Max both grabbed for Lia, but she was too quick. She kicked up out of her seat and shot from the cockpit, snatching the stunstick as she went and pulling off her Amphibio mask.

The hatch shut behind her and Max heard the whir of the airlock filling with water. Max watched in horror through the viewing screen as Lia darted up through the ocean onto Kull's massive, armoured back, then turned to face the aquafly, her eyes shining with triumph.

"Quick! Move!" the Professor shouted. Max gunned the engines and steered sharp right, but Kull flexed its giant body and surged towards them. Its long antennae lashed, hitting the aquafly with a loud crack and a flash of blue light. Max felt the whole craft judder. The lights on the dashboard flickered and the aquafly started to plummet, then lurched upwards again as the thrusters reengaged. Max jammed the thrust lever forwards, steering up the side of the volcano, away from the giant creature. He could see Kull in his rear viewer, following close behind. Lia sat astride its broad back, her face contorted with hatred, as Kull's antenna flicked towards them again.

Crash! Max felt the aquafly's engines stutter and the thrusters stall as Kull's energy bolt crackled around them, filling the cockpit with blinding blue light. As the light faded, the aquafly's engines growled back into life. The craft leapt forwards, but the displays were dim and Max could hear the engines struggling.

"Hit bad, Max!" Rivet barked.

"You're right, Riv!" Max said. "The aquafly can't take much more of this. It's time to fight back." Max took a deep breath, and slammed the aquafly around to face the Robobeast. He flicked switches and jabbed in commands, aiming all his blasters and acid torpedoes towards the creature's shell at once. *That should do it…* He let fly.

Boom! Max gaped in horror as his energy bullets fizzled away harmlessly where they hit Kull's armoured body. The green acid from the aquafly's torpedoes dribbled off without leaving a mark. Max spun the aquafly away from the Robobeast, and hit the accelerators. Lia whooped with glee as the trilobite swooped after the aquafly, letting out another searing stream of blue energy.

Crack! The aquafly's control screens flickered again and Max's teeth clashed together. The craft shuddered and dipped sharply towards the volcano's side. Max tugged on the controls, pulling them away from the craggy rock, but that took them straight back into the trilobite's path.

"This is hopeless!" Max told the Professor, steering right and left to try and shake the Robobeast. "We can't outrun it, and we can't fight it. There has to be some way to defeat that thing. You made it. What do we do?"

The Professor flinched as another bolt of electricity hit the craft, making it judder. Max noticed that his uncle was looking quite ill. His face was grey and covered with sweat, and as he glanced at Kull in the rear viewer, he swallowed hard.

"Well?" Max said.

"There might be a slight problem there,"

the Professor answered, his voice cracking with fear. "I chose Kull to protect my lab because, as a natural inhabitant of the Sea of Fire, it's basically bomb-proof. Which was perfect when it was mine, but is obviously rather less than ideal now."

Max felt frustration welling up inside him as he pushed the aquafly onwards as fast as its damaged engines would go. "Brilliant!" he said. It was all he could do to stop himself screaming with rage at his uncle. The Professor had built an invincible Robobeast, then let it get stolen by his crazy son. How stupid could one man possibly be? But then Max had a thought. *If there's one thing fighting the Professor has taught me, it's that there's no such thing as invincible robotics. Kull might be bomb-proof, but his wires and circuits won't be.*

"I'm going out there with Rivet," Max told

his uncle. "I'm going to destroy that thing's control systems."

"Don't be absurd!" the Professor snapped. "I've buried the command unit under its armour. You won't get to it whatever you do."

"Well, I'm going to try!" Max said. "Otherwise we're all going to get fried by your lame-brained invention. You keep it distracted, and I'll find its weakness." Before the Professor could argue, Max took hold of Rivet by the waist and hit the aquafly's emergency escape. His stomach flipped as he and his dogbot were shot out into the ocean through a hatch in the floor of the craft. Max glanced up to see the aquafly zoom away with Kull's massive, ancient form shooting after it.

"Rivet!" Max cried. "Take me up over Kull. I need to get a good look at its armour."

"Yes, Max!" Rivet barked. His propellers

whirred and Max held tight as the dogbot zoomed towards Kull, then up over the trilobite's colossal body. As Max raced past Lia, she smirked and pulled another energy pistol from a pouch in her tunic.

"Lia, don't!" Max shouted, but her finger was already pressing the trigger.

Zap! Max felt searing heat brush his cheek as Lia's energy bolt just missed.

Zap! She fired again and Rivet jerked out of the bolt's path, yanking Max through the water. Max looked down at Kull's armour, trying to concentrate despite the current whooshing past him, and Lia's constant hail of bullets. Rivet was swimming at full speed, racing to keep pace with Kull as the giant creature chased the aquafly up the mountain. Max scanned the creature's back, but could only see plates of shiny shell interlocking smoothly beneath him, and Lia, already taking aim again. There were no cracks or chinks in Kull's armour at all.

ZAP! Lia fired, and Rivet jerked Max out of her energy bullet's path just as the water around them sparked blue. Kull's long antennae had sent another arc of energy towards the aquafly speeding ahead.

BANG! The electric bolt hit the lightweight craft, which dropped like a stone. Max watched in dismay as the aquafly smashed into the craggy mountainside, then tumbled over and over until it came to rest in a crevice. He could see the Professor inside scrabbling at the controls, but the displays were all blank and the engines were silent. Kull cannoned towards the craft, its antennae already starting to crackle as they recharged for a final strike.

"Rivet! Quick!" Max said. "We need to lure Kull away from the aquafly or the Robobeast will kill the Professor!"

"Yes, Max!" Rivet barked. Max swam onto Rivet's back, and the dogbot shot forwards so fast Max's stomach was left behind. They soared alongside Kull, past the row of armoured spikes that ran along the trilobite's side. Lia let out an evil cackle of delight as they came within range of her pistol, and sent a stream of blaster fire towards them.

I'm beginning to wish I hadn't taught her to use that thing! Max thought, flattening himself against Rivet's metal body to avoid the deadly energy bolts. As Rivet raced onwards, past Kull's huge, black eye, Max saw a flash of triumph kindle in its inky, ancient depths.

"Kull's seen us!" Max told Rivet. "Lead it up over the volcano. We can hide in the metal debris on the other side."

"Got it, Max!" Rivet barked. Rivet's motors whirred as he soared up the mountainside.

"Where do you think you're going?" Lia screeched, sending more blaster fire their way as Kull swooped up the slope after them. The higher Rivet climbed, slaloming left and right between outcrops of rock, the hotter it became. Lia's energy bolts were still flying thick and fast, and, as Max glanced back, he could see Kull's long antennae reaching towards them. Max clenched his muscles and leaned low over Rivet's back, expecting to feel a zap of electricity, or the sharp sting of an energy blast at any moment.

Finally, Rivet shot up over the lip of the volcano. Max looked into the crater's fiery depths. Far below, half hidden by plumes of steam, black, bubbling rock swirled and churned, giving glimpses of the red-hot lava underneath. Max could taste an acidic tang in the water, and it stung as he drew it over his gills. "We have to get over the top of the volcano and down the other side – fast!" he told Rivet.

"Yes, Max!" Rivet barked. As the dogbot sped onwards, hot, sulphurous water streamed upwards past Max, along with bubbles of stinking gas. The heat and fumes made Max's head spin. He looked back to see Kull's vast, curved head forging onwards, and its long antennae reaching out.

Suddenly a sizzling bolt of blue energy lashed toward Rivet.

"Look out, Riv!"

SMACK! Pain fizzed through Max's hands and legs wherever they touched Rivet's metal body. Rivet's legs kicked wildly and his body shook. *He's been hit!* Rivet let out a whimper and started to tumble into the heart of the volcano. Max clung to his dogbot's back, gasping for breath as black rock whizzed past in a blur and boiling lava rose up to meet them.

"Rivet! Run diagnostics!" Max cried, his voice swept upwards by the buffeting water.

Rivet's eyes blinked as he ran the check. "Broken, Max!" he barked.

"I know that!" Max said. The water was getting hotter by the moment and plumes of choking gases were making his eyes and throat sting. "What's broken?"

"Thrusters, Max!" Rivet barked. Max immediately leaned over the dogbot as they both tumbled downwards. He flipped the panel in Rivet's side and peered into the dogbot's workings. He blinked, trying to clear his vision as his fingers traced the familiar lines of the components, looking for the fault. All the while, he could hear Lia cackling with laughter above them. He glanced up to see Kull waiting, just above the lip of the volcano. High on the creature's back, Lia had a ringside view of the action. *She could so easily help us...* Max thought. But he couldn't think about that. He turned his full attention back to Rivet's circuits.

"Going to crash, Max!" Rivet barked.

"Don't worry, Riv, I'm on it!" Max said, scanning the components. *Yes! There it is.* A wire had melted, causing a short. Max quickly rejigged the circuit. It was a messy fix, but it would have to do. As Max restored the connection, Rivet's thrusters spluttered into life. Max shut Rivet's side panel, dizzy with relief as the dogbot turned sharply away from the scalding lava below, and powered upwards.

But Max's relief quickly turned to alarm. Kull's eyes were shining with reflected fire, and Lia's lips spread slowly into a wicked grin as she met Max's gaze. Before Max and Rivet were halfway up the crater's side, Kull shot forwards, half covering the mouth of the volcano, then dipped his huge head downwards. The creature's legs and tail swept through the water and its massive body plunged towards Max and Rivet. The dogbot dodged out of the creature's path, but Kull swerved after him.

Smash! The creature's colossal body

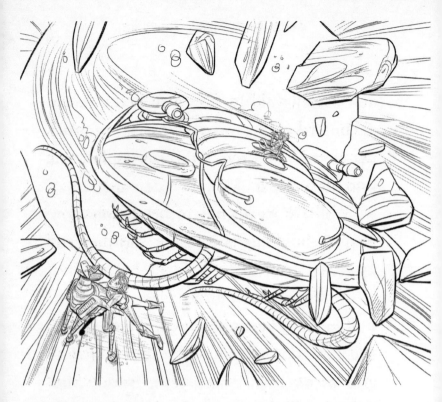

slammed against the crater side like a tanker
hitting an island. A deep, ominous rumble
echoed through the rock, and Max felt
vibrations in the water all around him. He
glanced down to see the lake of lava below
heaving with orange bubbles.

"Take cover, Riv!" Max cried, just as plumes
of steam erupted up from the depths with a
terrific hiss. Max and Rivet cowered against

the volcano's side as lava spewed up around them and cooled to chunks of hot black pumice. Max's eyes and gills were burning and his throat felt raw.

"We have to get out of here!" Max told Rivet, shouting above the hissing and bubbling below. "Kull might be built for this kind of environment, but we're not!" Suddenly, he had the spark of an idea. *Kull's built to withstand lava, but the Professor's robotics can't be! And if he hits the sides hard enough...* Max glanced at the roiling lava below, imagining the force of a full-blown eruption.

It was a desperate plan. Possibly deadly. But it might just work.

CHAPTER SEVEN

A FATAL DOSE

"Behind that outcrop!" Max called to Rivet, pointing towards a ridge below them in the crater's side.

"Hot, Max!" Rivet barked.

"Trust me, Riv," Max said. "We're going to get out of here. Just do as I say."

Rivet's propellers whirred and Max felt his skin tingle as they headed deeper into the heart of the volcano. He just hoped Rivet could withstand the heat. As he glanced upwards, he saw Kull's huge eyes bearing down on them from above, shining like pits of fire.

Rivet ducked behind the jutting outcrop of black volcanic rock, and Max peered out to see Kull getting closer. Lia was frowning as she ran her eyes over the walls of the volcano, watching for them to emerge. "When I say *go*," Max told Rivet, "full throttle up and out, okay?"

"Got it, Max!" Rivet said.

Max waited, his nerves taut and his pulse racing. Finally, when Kull was so close Max could feel the hairs on his arms starting to tingle with the ancient creature's electricity, Max swam onto Rivet's back. "Go, Riv!" he cried.

Rivet's engines throbbed and Max held tight as they rocketed up. Lia screeched with rage as Max shot past towards the mouth of the volcano. Max glanced back to see Kull arc its gigantic body, swoop over the bubbling lava below, then lift its head to climb up the crater's other side. But the Robobeast was far too big to do a U-turn inside the volcano. Its massive head smashed into the rock of the crater with a sickening crunch. The whole volcano shuddered and gave a deep, rumbling roar that shook Max to the core. Lia's eyes opened wide and her arms and legs flailed as she was flung from Kull's back. Kull curled its massive body into a shiny armoured ball, and together, Lia and Kull plummeted towards the churning lava.

"Full power to Lia!" Max called to his dogbot. Rivet turned and sped towards Lia as the lava below them rippled and churned. Max could sense the energy building in the rock all around him. He could feel the heat becoming fiercer. They didn't have long, but Lia was falling like a stone. Her face was calm and blank as her hair fluttered about her. She wasn't even trying to swim. *Siborg's letting her fall to her death!* Max realised. *Well, not on my watch.* He gritted his teeth and willed Rivet onwards, faster towards his friend. As soon as Max was close enough, he reached out and grabbed Lia by the wrist. She turned to him with a look of rage, and tried to tug her

arm free, but Max pulled her towards him, wrapping her in a bear hug. "Go, Rivet!" Max cried, clinging to Rivet's back with his knees as the dogbot climbed through the water.

Max glanced downwards just as Kull's huge, curled body plunged into the magma below, throwing up a plume of molten rock. *This is it!* Max tensed his muscles and gritted his teeth. *I just hope we get out in time!* Hissing clouds of steam filled with chunks of black rock and red lava shot past Max's face as Rivet's engines whined. The noise was tremendous and Max's eardrums felt like they would explode. Hot currents buffeted Rivet from side to side. Max's every breath burned his gills. *Almost there...* Lia was pounding at Max with her fists, trying to get free, but he held her tight as they climbed upwards through the treacherous water.

Finally, they reached the lip of the volcano.

Rivet managed a final burst of speed and tugged them out into the open ocean.

BOOM!

Behind them, a huge eruption of lava, rock and steam exploded outwards into the sea. The whole ocean floor trembled as Rivet dived behind a rock, protecting them from

the deadly rain of glowing pumice that was pattering down all around them.

Max and Lia fell to the seabed, breathless and dizzy with the heat and the toxic fumes. Rivet crouched down beside them. The groaning of the eruption went on and on. *I hope the Professor managed to find somewhere to hide!* Max thought.

After what seemed like an age, the earth finally stopped shaking. Max glanced out from behind the rock, and gasped at the strange contorted shapes of cooled black lava that had transformed the seascape. A guilty uneasiness grew inside him as the volcano steamed silently. *I hope the Professor was right about Kull's armour*, he thought. *I'd hate to think that ancient creature was dead.*

As Max stared at the clouds of steam billowing from the mouth of the volcano, he saw them swirl and eddy around, as if something huge was stirring inside. Then Kull's shiny, armoured body shot out of the swirling haze. Max scanned Kull's curved antennae for any trace of the electronics that had trapped the beast, but the shimmering blue wires were gone, burned away in the heat of the eruption. The giant creature flexed its armoured body, swooped overhead, and darted away. *He's free!*

ZAP! A thousand points of burning pain shot through Max. His vision blurred, his knees buckled and he crumpled to the seabed, his body prickling and fizzing. Somehow he forced his screaming limbs to move, and scrambled onto his back.

Lia was standing over him, her pistol held in one hand, and the Professor's stunstick in the other. Rivet barked and leapt towards her, but without even turning, Lia aimed the stunstick and fired. The dogbot was thrown backwards, blue energy crackling around his body and his limbs jerking wildly.

Lia's eyes were wild with rage and her teeth clenched together as she spoke. "I am sick of your meddling!" she said in Siborg's robotic tones. "Why won't you just die?" Lia glanced at a dial on the side of the stunstick. "Fatal dose," she read. Then her fingers reached for the dial and turned. Max watched helplessly, his body tingling and trembling as she turned the stunstick towards him.

"Lia! Please! No!" Max cried. But there wasn't a trace of pity or friendship in Lia's crazed stare.

Max saw a flicker of movement from behind her. At the base of the volcano, amid the curling formation of new volcanic rock, something was stirring. Max's heart leapt. It was the Professor, emerging from the aquafly with his mindbug raygun in his hand. As the Professor's gaze fell on Max and Lia, he blinked, then quickly opened the side of the raygun and started tinkering. *I have to buy him time!* Max realised. *I have to stall Siborg.*

Max looked into Lia's eyes. "So, cousin!" he said, in the sternest voice his trembling body could manage. "Are you really so afraid of me that you need to get Lia to do your dirty work? Surely it's time we faced each other man to man?"

Lia laughed and curled her lip into a sneer. "I'm not going to play your games, Max," she said, as she drew back her arm. Max summoned every scrap of his returning strength and whipped his hyperblade from his belt. He slashed it forwards, smashing the stunstick aside. The pain of the impact ran along his arm, but Lia was already swinging for him again.

"Die!" she screamed. Max rolled, dodging

the blow, which crackled against the seabed beside him. Lia lifted her arm once more. The stunstick rushed towards him. Max swung his blade, knocking the stunstick aside, but his parry was clumsy and his fingers were numb and tingling. He lost his grip on the hilt, and his blade went spinning through the water. Max tried to scramble back out of reach, but he hit a ledge of rock behind him. And there was no way he could outswim Lia. Even without her enhanced strength, Max knew that the Merryn princess was far quicker than he was underwater.

He tensed his muscles against the final blow. "Lia! If you're in there you need to listen!" he cried. "It's me! Max!"

But Lia had a hideous grin of victory painted across her face. Max threw his arms up to shield his face, knowing it wouldn't save him.

ZAP! There was a tremendous flash and Lia froze, hit by a shot from the Professor's raygun. A white halo of light surrounded her stricken form. Her eyes went wide with fear. In the brief moment before she sank to the ocean floor, Max caught a glimpse of the Lia he knew, confused and terrified. He scrambled to his feet and raced to her side as Rivet bounded over and started nudging her face with his nose.

"Lia? Are you all right?" Max cried.

"Wake up!" Rivet barked. But Lia lay motionless, her eyes closed and her mouth slightly open. Her silver hair was spread across the black seabed and she looked as if she was sleeping. Except that Max couldn't see any movement at all. Not even the flickering of the gills at her neck. A jolt of horror stabbed through his body.

She's not breathing!

CHAPTER EIGHT

INTO BATTLE

"Lia!" Max grabbed his fallen friend by the shoulders and shook her lifeless form. The Professor arrived at his side, holding the finished raygun in his hand.

"What have you done?" Max shouted at his uncle, anguish flooding through him.

The Professor smiled smugly and patted his gun. "I saved your life," he said. Then he glanced at Lia and frowned. "Maybe you should stop shaking the young lady. Her teeth are starting to rattle." At that moment

Lia let out a groan, and Max saw the gills at her neck start to flutter. Her eyes flickered open and Max could tell at once that his friend was back.

"Lia!" he said, gently laying her down. "I'm so glad you're okay."

"Where am I?" Lia muttered sleepily.

"The Sea of Fire," Max said. Rivet started licking Lia's face, his tail wagging madly. Lia sat up and gently pushed the dogbot away, frowning in confusion. "You were bitten by a mindbug," Max said. "But you're okay now."

"Oh!" Lia suddenly looked horrified. "I thought it was all a dream. I kept trying to wake up but I couldn't… I shot at you!"

Max cut her off with a wave of his hand. "Don't worry about it," he said, "I know it wasn't you. It was Siborg acting through his evil mindbug. I'm just glad you're okay."

"But where's Spike?" Lia asked, glancing

around quickly. "I thought he was with you!"

"He swam off," Max said. "I think he went looking for you. Don't worry, I promise we'll find him. But first we need to fix the aquafly so we can go and defeat Siborg."

"With my quite brilliantly effective and not remotely deadly raygun," the Professor said, waving the gun. "I can't believe you doubted me, Max. And more to the point, I can't believe you broke Kull. If you hadn't set that old fossil free, we'd be able to use it to defeat my son."

"Kull deserves to be free!" Max said, shooting the Professor a look which must have been even more furious than he'd intended.

The Professor took a step back and held up his hands defensively. "It was just a thought," he said. Then his face went deathly pale. "And you have to admit," he said, his voice suddenly high and tight, "Kull would have been extremely useful against all those evil robots over there." The Professor pointed.

Max followed the line of the Professor's finger, and his stomach sank. Emerging from behind a rock was a swarm of glowing red eyes. And he could just make out the scrawny black bodies they belonged to. *Cyrates. At least fifty of them.*

"Take cover! Quick!" Max cried. He held out a hand to Lia, but she shook her head.

"I'm fine now," she said, flicking her arms and legs and swimming up beside him. Max scanned the new rock formations around the base of the volcano, looking for a hiding place. He spotted a boulder, streaked with black and grey lines. "Over there!" he said. Max, Lia and the Professor darted towards the rock with Rivet swimming alongside them. When Max reached the cover of the boulder, he lifted his head and peered out.

"So, what's the plan?" the Professor asked, peeking over the rock beside Max. Max bit his lip as he watched the cyrates approach. *There are so many of them!* Max glanced at the Professor and Lia. Between them, they had one pistol, one stunstick, one hyperblade, and Rivet's teeth…against what looked like fifty of the cyrates' blasters.

"If we could reach the aquafly," Max said, swallowing the terror that was rising in his throat, "I should be able to get it up and running. Then we'd have its blasters and acid torpedoes. Maybe you guys could keep the cyrates busy for long enough for me to fix it?"

But even as Max said the words, he knew he was clutching at straws. He could hear the hum of the cyrates' rocket boots getting louder by the moment. *We don't stand a chance!* Max thought. *I can't believe we've got the raygun working and saved Lia, only to be defeated now!* His mind flicked to a picture of his parents, back in Aquora, living with Siborg as their son. Forever.

"Max!" Lia cut into his train of thought. She was smiling, and her eyes shone. "Listen!"

Max cocked his head, and above the

hideous drone of the cyrates' rockets he could hear fierce shouts and the clang of metal on metal. *A battle!*

Together, Max and Lia looked out over the rock, and what Max saw filled him with joy.

A swarm of Merryn soldiers riding swordfish had surrounded the cyrates and were hacking at them with long spears and glinting blades. The tallest and broadest of the warriors was wearing a coral crown.

"Father!" Lia cried. She lifted her stunstick and sped out from behind the rock. Max followed her, hyperblade in hand, and Rivet powered after him.

"Probably best if I just wait here, then?" Max heard the Professor mutter as they all swam away.

ZAP! Lia brought her stunstick down on a cyrate's metal skull. The cyrate sizzled and sparked, then dropped like a stone, its r

eyes dark. Several of the evil robots spun
in the water to face Max and Lia. Others
fired energy bolts at their Merryn attackers,
but the warriors caught the blasts on pearl
shields, and kept hacking away at the robots.
A cyrate aimed its blaster at Max's chest,
and Max swung his hyperblade, slicing off
the robot's arm. He sent his blade swishing
through the water again, and the cyrate fell,

its head severed from its shoulders.

More cyrates poured towards Max and Lia. Max's blade flickered, and Lia's stunstick let off zap after zap of electricity. Rivet growled, his teeth tearing arms and legs from the evil, red-eyed robots. Max felt energy flowing through his limbs as cyrates fell before him. All around him, Merryn warriors shouted and their weapons sang. Soon the swish of blades through water died away and the sound of blaster fire fell silent.

Max looked around for more red eyes to fight. But there were no cyrates left, just strong Merryn men and women, raising their spears in victory as piles of robotic body parts smoked silently on the black volcanic slopes.

Lia swooped through the water towards her father and threw her arms around his neck. "You rescued us! How did you know we needed you?"

King Salinus peeled Lia from his neck and smiled down at his daughter. "Well, I just happened to be on a hunting trip not far from here, when I heard a familiar clicking sound. Then who do you think should come zooming towards us from behind a clump of weed?" He paused for dramatic effect while Lia waited, her face full of worry and hope. "Only Spike!" the king went on. "He was in a terrible state and insisted we come at once. And I have to say, he had me rather worried. He said you were sick."

A trill of merry clicks echoed through the water. "Spike!" Lia cried, twirling to face her swordfish as he sped out from behind a Merryn soldier.

When Spike reached his mistress, he pressed his cheek against hers, and Lia closed her eyes, smiling with joy as she nuzzled against him.

"Hi, Spike!" Rivet barked, his tail wagging happily. Spike shook his fin in response.

Max reached out a hand and patted the swordfish's back. "He must have sensed your hunting party and gone for help," Max told King Salinus. "Clever Spike!" Spike lifted his head and let out another trill, his eyes sparkling proudly as Max stroked his dorsal fin.

CHAPTER NINE

WHATEVER IT TAKES

"That should do it!" the Professor said, slamming the aquafly's engine compartment shut.

"Here's hoping," Max said, wiping his oily hands on his deepsuit, "but we won't know for sure until we power her up." He swam up into the open cockpit, passing through the airlock. "Fingers crossed," he said, and hit the engines. The aquafly whirred into life, and Max felt a rush of relief. He ran his eyes across the cockpit displays, and tapped in a command to run a diagnostic check.

"All systems functional," the aquafly's mechanical voice said through Max's headset. Max threw the Professor the thumbs up, and the Professor gave him a smug grin in return.

"So, can we finally get going?" Lia asked, seated on Spike's back next to the sub. Max couldn't help grinning at the exasperation in her voice. She was definitely back to her old self. Beside her, King Salinus was waiting with his host of Merryn warriors, ready to accompany them back to Aquora to face Siborg.

"Just about," Max said. He rummaged under his dashboard and pulled out Lia's Spear. "Riv," Max said, "take this to Lia!" Rivet gripped the spear in his mouth and zoomed to Spike's side.

Lia smiled as she took hold of her spear. "It feels good to get that back!" she said. "I don't think I'll ever feel the same about firing a pistol again." Lia shuddered suddenly, her smile gone, and Max could see she was struggling with her memories of being controlled by Siborg. "But anyway," she said at last, smiling once more, "we've got a city full of people to save. Not least your mum and dad. Let's get out of here!"

"Max!" King Salinus called. "A quick word before we go, if you don't mind." Max bowed his head, then swam out of the aquafly and over to the Merryn king.

"Must your uncle join us on our return to Aquora?" Salinus asked, casting a sideways glance at the Professor, who was polishing scorch-marks from the aquafly's hood. "Do you really believe we can trust him?"

Max frowned. "I'm not sure trust is the right word," he said. "But for now at least, we're on the same side. Siborg wants his father dead along with all of us. Plus, so far, the Professor has kept his word. He saved my life, and freed Lia from Siborg's mindbug."

Salinus nodded, but his forehead was creased into deep furrows. "It is not possible that the Professor will defect once he's helped us defeat his son?"

Max nodded. "I'm almost sure of it," he said. "But for the moment, we've no choice but to take him with us." Max lifted the raygun to show Salinus. "This works, but only on one person at a time. We're going to need his help if we're to have any hope of freeing everyone in Aquora."

Salinus gave another uneasy nod. "In that case, let us proceed," he said, "but I will be keeping a close watch on that man, and I expect you to do the same."

Max bowed again, and darted back towards the aquafly. The Professor and Rivet had climbed inside, and Lia was hovering nearby on Spike. Max swam up into his seat and closed the cockpit.

"Let's go!" Max cried, gunning the engines. The aquafly zoomed forwards, followed

by King Salinus with Lia, and their host of
Merryn warriors.

As they surged away from the bleak
seascape of the Sea of Fire, Max felt a familiar
stirring in his gut. He had defeated Kull. He
had the power of Merryn warriors and the
Professor's technical knowledge on his side.

But still, the coils of dread were back, twisting and writhing. *Mum and Dad are depending on me, along with everyone else in Aquora.* He took a deep breath and squared his shoulders, then glanced back at the raygun where it lay safely in the aquafly.

Whatever it takes, he told himself, *I'm going to defeat Siborg.*

Once and for all.

Don't miss Max's next Sea Quest adventure,

when he faces

GULAK
THE GULPER EEL

SEA QUEST ®

Look out for all the books in
Sea Quest Series 7:

THE LOST STARSHIP

VELOTH THE VAMPIRE SQUID

GLENDOR THE STEALTHY SHADOW

MIRROC THE GOBLIN SHARK

BLISTRA THE SEA DRAGON

OUT IN MARCH 2016!

Don't miss the
BRAND NEW
Special Bumper Edition:
JANDOR
THE ARCTIC LIZARD

OUT IN NOVEMBER 2015

WIN AN EXCLUSIVE GOODY BAG

In every Sea Quest book the Sea Quest logo is
hidden in one of the pictures. Find the logos in books
21-24, make a note of which pages they appear on and
go online to enter the competition at

www.seaquestbooks.co.uk

Each month we will put all of the correct entries into a draw
and select one winner to receive a special Sea Quest goody bag.

You can also send your entry on a postcard to:

Sea Quest Competition, Orchard Books,
Carmelite House, 50 Victoria Embankment,
London, EC4Y 0DZ

Don't forget to include your name and address!

GOOD LUCK

Closing Date: Dec 30th 2015

IF YOU LIKE SEA QUEST, YOU'LL LOVE BEAST QUEST!

Series 1: COLLECT THEM ALL!

An evil wizard has enchanted the magical beasts of Avantia. Only a true hero can free the beasts and save the land. Is Tom the hero Avantia has been waiting for?

FERNO
THE FIRE DRAGON
978 1 84616 483 5

SEPRON
THE SEA SERPENT
978 1 84616 482 8

ARCTA
THE MOUNTAIN GIANT
978 1 84616 484 2

TAGUS
THE HORSE-MAN
978 1 84616 486 6

NANOOK
THE SNOW MONSTER
978 1 84616 485 9

EPOS
THE FLAME BIRD
978 1 84616 487 3

DON'T MISS THE
BRAND NEW SERIES OF:

Series 15: VELMAL'S REVENGE

WARDOK
THE SKY TERROR

978 1 40833 487 4

XERIK
THE BONE CRUNCHER

978 1 40833 489 8

PLEXOR
THE RAGING REPTILE

978 1 40833 491 1

QUAGOS
THE ARMOURED BEETLE

978 1 40833 493 5

COMING SOON